THE USBORNE SOCCER SCHOOL
PASSING AND SHOOTING

Gill Harvey

Designed by Stephen Wright
Photographs by Chris C...
Illustrations by Bob B...

Edited by Cheryl Evans; Cover Design by Tom Lalonde;
Digital Imaging by John Russell; Consultant: John Shiels,
Bobby Charlton International Soccer Schools Ltd.

Library photographs: Allsport UK; Cover photograph: Bartlomiej Zborowski/epa/Corbis

With special thanks to soccer players Brooke Astle, David Buckley,
James Peter Greatrex, Gemma Grimshaw, Sarah Leigh, John Jackson,
Christopher Sharples, Jody Spence, Christopher White and to their coach, Bryn Cooper

CONTENTS

ABOUT THIS BOOK

This book looks at the kicking, heading and team skills that you need to pass or shoot well, with plenty of games and exercises to help you improve. Here you can find out about the soccer terms that you will come across as you read.

PARTS OF THE FOOT

These are the parts of your feet you use most often for passing and shooting. You rarely use your heel or sole.

The **inside** of your foot is from your big toe back to your ankle.

Your **instep** is the area over your laces. It doesn't include your toes.

The **outside** of your foot is from your little toe back to your ankle.

'OVER THE BALL'

Your position 'over the ball' refers to how far forward or back you are leaning. It is important because it affects how powerful and how high your kick will be. If your head is over the ball, your kick is more likely to stay low, and it may be more accurate, too.

This player is well balanced, with his head over the ball.

WHERE TO KICK THE BALL

You make the ball go in different directions by knowing which part of it to kick. To work out which part is which, think of it as having two sides, a top and a bottom. The diagrams below show how this will be illustrated throughout the book.

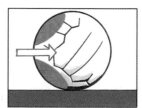

When you are told to kick one side of the ball, you see a diagram of it as it looks from above when you kick. Kick to the left or right.

The book shows the top or bottom of the ball by looking at it side on, so imagine what it would look like from the side as you kick.

When you are told to kick the ball through the middle, this means both the middle from above and the middle from the side.

From above, you see the right side.

From the side, you see the middle.

If you are told just one part of the ball to kick, for example the right side, you can assume you kick through the middle from the other angle.

BACKSWING AND FOLLOW-THROUGH

Your **'backswing'** means the action of swinging your leg back before kicking.

Your **'follow-through'** is when you swing your leg forward and up after kicking.

The backswing

The follow-through

USING BOTH FEET

Although the book does not remind you on every page, you should practise all the techniques and exercises with both feet. If you can only play well with one foot, you have to waste time moving the ball into a good position before playing it away. This can mean that you miss good chances to pass or shoot.

This left-footed pass sends the ball to the right.

SOCCER TERMS

This book does not use a lot of soccer terms, but there are a few which you do need to know. The **'attacking third'** means the final third of the pitch, where you approach your opponents' goal.
The **'defending third'** is where you protect your goal from opponents.

This is the red team's defending third.

In this book, an **attacker** is any player in a team which has the ball. A **defender** is any player in a team which doesn't have the ball.

DISGUISE, PACE AND TIMING

Giving a kick **disguise** means making it difficult to guess which way it will go.

The **pace** of the ball is how fast it is going. If a ball 'has pace', it is going fast.

Good **timing** means judging the best time to hit the ball when you pass or shoot.

This is the red team's attacking third and the yellow team's defending third.

INSIDE FOOT KICKS

The inside of your foot is the area you use most often for kicking. It has a larger kicking surface than any other part of your foot. This makes it easier for you to judge how the ball will respond when you kick it, so it is ideal for accurate passes.

THE PUSH PASS

This is a low kick for short distances. It is called a pass, but you can use it to shoot at close range. It is easy to learn, and accurate.

Non-kicking foot

Kicking foot

1. Swing your foot back, turning it out so that it is almost at right angles to your other foot.

2. Keep your ankle firm and your body over your feet. Make contact with the middle of the ball.

3. Follow through in a smooth, level movement, keeping your eye on the ball the whole time. Keep your foot low - try not to sweep it upwards, as this will make the ball rise.

ACCURACY PRACTICE

Work with a friend. Place two markers 60cm (2ft) apart. One of you stands 1m (3ft) in front of them, the other 1m (3ft) behind. Try to pass to each other through the gap. Score a point for each success.

After five passes each, move another 1m (3ft) apart and start again. Carry on until you are 10m (30ft) apart. The player with the most points wins.

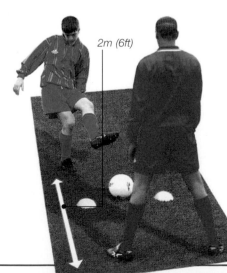

2m (6ft)

HOW TO MEASURE

Measurements for all the exercises and games in this book are given in metres (m) and feet (ft). Exact distances are not important, so think of 1m (3ft) as about one big stride. You can then measure out the right area in strides.

THE INSIDE FOOT SWERVE

Swerving the ball is really useful when passing or shooting. You have more control with the inside of your foot than the outside, so it is best to learn the inside foot swerve first.

Direction of ball

Kicking foot

Non-kicking foot

The ball should swerve out, then swing back in again.

Follow through freely, your foot rising to follow the direction of the ball.

1. Keep your eyes on the ball as you swing your leg back. Your non-kicking foot should be well out of the way of the ball.

2. Use the side of your foot to kick. The secret is to kick the ball in the right place. (See above).

PIG IN THE MIDDLE

Play this game with two friends. Stand in a line with 10m (30ft) between you. The player in the middle cannot move more than 60cm (2ft) to either side. The players at each end try to bend the ball around the player in the middle. If he is able to intercept it, the player who kicked it takes his place.

Mark out your positions so that you can't cheat.

10m (30ft)

60cm (2ft)

STAR PUSH PASS

This picture shows Romanian player Dan Petrescu following through a push pass. See how his foot is still level and low, and how his weight is balanced over his knees.

OUTSIDE FOOT KICKS

When you use the outside of your foot to kick the ball, you can disguise your movements very well. Also, because the ball is to one side of you, you are able to move freely and pass or shoot as you run. However, accuracy and control can be difficult, so you will need to practise hard.

FLICKING THE BALL TO THE SIDE

FLICK GAME

This move is particularly useful when you are under pressure and you receive a fast pass from the side which you do not have time to control. The trick is to let the ball bounce off the outside of your foot, while at the same time directing it to a team-mate with a flick of your ankle.

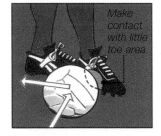

Make contact with little toe area.

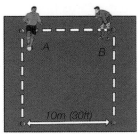

A B

10m (30ft)

This is for two players (A and B). Mark out a 10m (30ft) square. Start in the two top corners.

You don't need any backswing.

1. Keep your back to anyone marking you. Turn the outside of your foot towards the ball.

2. Don't cushion the ball as it makes contact. Direct it out to the side with a flick of your foot.

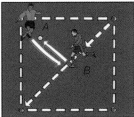

A

B

B runs across the square as A passes the ball into his path. B returns it with a flick pass.

3. If the ball has been kicked through the middle, it should stay low but fast. Try to direct it into the path of another player.

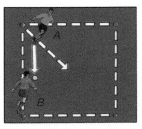

A

B

This player can see a team-mate out of the corner of his eye.

This player has no chance of reaching the ball.

A pushes the ball to B, then starts to run. B feeds the ball for him to flick back. Carry on like this.

OUTSIDE FOOT SWERVES

This kick makes the ball swerve away to the side. It is a difficult kick to master, and you need to be quite strong to make it go a long way. However, you don't need to control the ball before you kick it and you can do it as you run, so it is an ideal kick to use for shots at goal.

Hit the ball half-way up if you want it to stay low.

Non-kicking foot

1. Swing your leg back. As you swing your foot back towards the ball, turn the toes of your kicking foot in slightly towards your other foot. Kick the inside of the ball with the area around your little toe.

2. Give the kick plenty of follow-through, sweeping your leg across your body. The ball should swerve out away from you.

Your non-kicking foot should be well out of the way of your kicking foot.

LOFTED SWERVES

A 'lofted kick means a high kick. If you want an outside foot swerve to go higher and clear other players, kick the ball through its lower half and not through the middle.

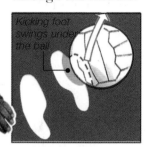

Kicking foot swings under the ball

PAIRS PRACTICE

Pass the ball down a straight line. Try to make it swing out from the line and back in again by using outside foot swerves.

Try standing further apart - 15m (45ft).

You can also practise outside foot swerves by playing 'Pig in the Middle' (see page 5).

USING YOUR INSTEP

Your instep is the area over your laces. It is the most powerful part of your foot, so use it if you want to kick the ball a long way or kick it very hard. At first you may accidentally use your toes, but this will improve with practice.

THE LOW INSTEP DRIVE

You can use this kick as you are running to send it a long way. It is quite difficult to make it accurate, but the secret of success is to hit the ball right through the middle.

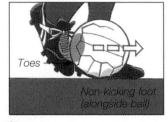

Toes

Non-kicking foot (alongside ball)

Place your non-kicking foot close to the ball.

1. Swing your kicking leg well back, so that your heel almost reaches up to your behind.

2. Point your toes toward the ground and make contact with the middle of the ball.

3. Swing your foot onwards in the direction of the ball, but make sure your ankle is still stretched out towards the ground as you follow through. This is the key to keeping the kick low.

INSTEP PASS GAME

Use this game to help you develop your basic instep kicking technique. It is best with four people, but you could play with any number above two - change the shape of the pitch to make a corner for each player.

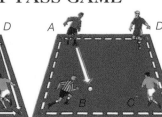

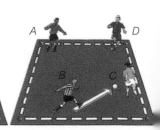

Mark out a 30m (90ft) square. Label yourselves A, B, C and D and stand at its four corners.

A passes to B at an angle so that he has to run on to it. B receives it and passes it at an angle to C.

After passing, B stays where he is. C runs on to the ball and passes to D, and so on around the square.

THE LOFTED DRIVE

The lofted drive is a long, high kick. The technique for doing it is similar to the technique for low instep kicks, but you kick the ball in a different place and let your foot swing right up when you follow through.

Kicking the ball on its lower half makes it rise.

1. Approach the ball from a slight angle. Swing your leg back, looking down at the ball as you do so.

2. Make contact with the lower half of the ball, so that your instep reaches slightly under it.

3. Follow through with a sweeping movement, letting your leg swing up across your body.

GAINING POWER AND HEIGHT

You will find that your drives will be higher and more powerful if you lean back as you swing your leg towards the ball. This usually happens naturally, though you may find it easier if you kick from slightly further away.

This player leans well back, showing his confidence in kicking the ball powerfully.

PERFECTING YOUR TECHNIQUE

To improve your lofted drives you may think you just need to kick the ball harder, but it is more important to develop your technique. In this game you practise drives that need to be accurate as well as powerful to reach their target.

Four of you (A, B, C, D) can work at this by marking out a row of four boxes, all 10m (30ft) square. Each of you stands in a box, which you cannot move out of.

A and B try to lob the ball over C and D. Score a point for each success. If C or D manages to intercept the ball, he takes the place of the player who kicked it.

D intercepts the ball and takes the place of A.

VOLLEYING

Volleying means kicking the ball before it has hit the ground. It is a fast and exciting way to play the ball, because you don't spend time controlling it before playing it. This gives the ball pace and makes it harder for your opponents to guess where it is going to go.

FRONT VOLLEY

Front volleys are probably the easiest volleys to do, but you still need quick reactions to do them well. You use your instep to receive the ball, so you need to be facing it. If you are not, it can be difficult to keep your balance and the volley may go out of control.

Kick through the lower half of the ball.

The ball makes contact with your instep.

1. Lift your knee as the ball approaches. Point your toes and stretch out your ankle.

If you make contact later, your non-kicking foot should be closer to the ball.

2. As you direct the ball away, try to keep your head forward over your knee.

LEARNING TO VOLLEY

Work with a friend. Stand 3m (10ft) apart. Drop the ball onto your foot and volley it to him gently for him to catch.

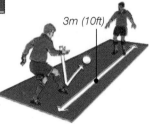

3m (10ft)

VARYING THE HEIGHT

If you want to send the ball high, perhaps to clear a defender, get your foot right under the ball.

To stop the ball rising too much, lift your foot up over the ball slightly after making contact.

SIDE VOLLEY

Side volleys are more difficult than front volleys. You need quick reactions, as you do for any volley, but the leg movement that you have to do is also quite tricky - you need to be able to balance on one leg while you are leaning sideways.

1. Watch the ball as it comes towards you so that you can judge the right angle to meet it.

2. As you lift your outside leg up, make sure that the shoulder nearest the ball isn't in the way.

3. Swing your leg up and round in a sideways movement so that your instep makes contact.

4. Follow through in the direction of the ball by swinging your leg right across your body.

HIGHER AND LOWER

If you want to keep the ball low, try to make contact with the ball just above the middle.

To make the ball rise over the heads of other players, kick it just below the middle.

SIDE ACTION PRACTICE

Because the leg movement is the most difficult part of this volley, you may find it helps to practise over an obstacle. Make or find something that is almost as high as your hip, and try swinging your leg over it. You can put the ball on top of it if you want. If it is too high to reach, begin with a lower obstacle.

TRIO VOLLEY GAME

When you can do the leg movement, play this with two friends. A throws the ball to B, who volleys to C. C throws the ball for A to volley, and so on.

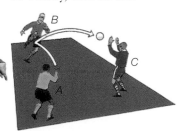

Score a point each time you volley accurately. The player with the most points after ten volleys each is the winner.

MORE ABOUT VOLLEYING

Much of the skill in volleying depends on having the confidence to strike the ball early. If you take the initiative and go for the ball instead of waiting for it to reach you, you will find it easier to control its direction. All the volleys on these pages are most effective if you act quickly and decisively.

THE HALF-VOLLEY

To do a half-volley, you kick the ball just as it bounces. If you kick it correctly, it should stay low and also be quite powerful. Point your toes, stretch out your ankle, then kick the ball with your instep. Your knee should make a firm snapping action.

Once it is kicked, the ball shoots off very fast.

Your non-kicking foot is alongside the ball and a little behind it.

1. Judge the flight of the ball and position yourself just behind where it will land. Take a short backswing.

2. Keeping your head forward so that it is in line with your knee, kick the ball as soon as it hits the ground.

VOLLEYS IN THE AIR

If the ball is very high, you may need to jump for it and volley it in the air.

Use a front or side volley technique, depending on the angle of the ball.

Your timing has to be especially good, so keep your eye on the ball all the time.

Watch the flight of the ball as you land. Get ready to follow the ball forward.

THE 'LAY-OFF' VOLLEY

'Laying the ball off' means playing the ball to another player when you don't have much time to play it yourself. To play a 'lay-off' volley, take the ball early and direct it out to the left or right with your first touch.

Instead of using your instep, turn your foot to use the inside or outside of it.

Make contact with the middle of the ball, or slightly above the middle to send the ball down.

Here, a defender is in a position to challenge the player receiving the ball. He can see that a team-mate is in a better position to play the ball forward, so he lays it off to him.

ONE BOUNCE GAME

In this game, you can make use of all the volleys you have learned. It is for three or more players, though it is best with about six. Each player begins with five lives.

10m (30ft)

Stand in a circle 10m (30ft) across. One player kicks the ball high to another player, who lets it bounce once then volleys it to someone else. Use any type of volley.

You lose a life for missing or mis-hitting a volley. The winner is the last with any lives left. Next, play without letting the ball bounce (apart from half-volleys).

STAR VOLLEY

Here, Alessandro del Piero of Italy jumps for a volley. Even though he is at full stretch, he is balanced and has his eye on the ball.

CHIPPING

The chip is a kick which makes the ball rise very quickly into the air. It is not very powerful, but it is ideal for lifting the ball over opponents' heads, especially the goalkeeper's.

Here, the player watches the ball as it rises up away from him.

BASIC TECHNIQUE

The secret of the chip is to stab at the ball without following through. The area just below your instep acts like a wedge which punches the ball into the air.

Direction of ball

1. Face the ball straight on. It is almost impossible to chip from the side. Take a short backswing.

2. Bring your foot down with a sharp stabbing action, aiming your foot at the bottom of the ball.

3. Your foot kicks into the ground as it hits the ball, which is why there is no follow-through. This should happen naturally - it doesn't really matter if your leg does swing up as long as the ball flies into the air.

TECHNIQUE TIPS

Your non-kicking foot should be alongside the ball and close to it, only about 20cm (4in) away.

Kicking foot

Vary your chips by leaning forward or back. If you lean back, the chip will not fly as high, but it may go further.

CHIPPING PRACTICE

You can chip the ball when it is still or when it is moving. It is probably easiest to do if you run on to the ball as it is moving towards you. This exercise allows you to practise your basic technique with the ball coming towards you.

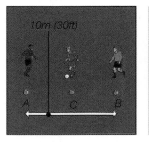

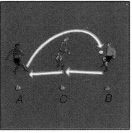

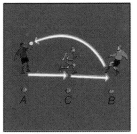

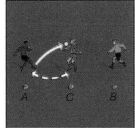

The exercise is for three players. Lay out three markers 10m (30ft) apart.

C passes along the ground to A. A chips it over C to B, who plays it back to C.

C plays the ball along the ground to B, who chips it to A. A passes it to C.

If A or B mis-hits a chip, he goes into the middle and C takes his place.

COMPARING HIGH KICKS

It is difficult to chip very far, so use a lofted drive for longer kicks. Here, you practise both types of kick. You need two or more players. Divide into two groups. Put six markers in a row, 5m (15ft) apart, and mark out a 5m (15ft) area around each one.

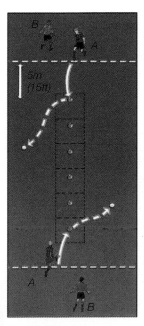

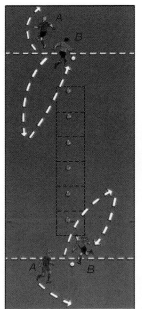

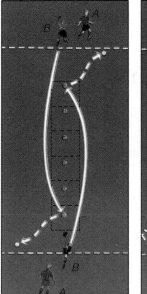

Stand 5m (15ft) from each end of the row. The first player tries to chip into the first area, aiming for the marker in the middle.

Score 10 for hitting the area, 20 for the marker. The next player gets the ball while you go to the back of the queue.

All of you try hitting the first area, then move on to the next. Use lofted drives for the last three areas, instead of chips.

To save running to collect the ball, pick up the opposite group's long drives. Keep playing, making a note of the score.

TRICK MOVES

Sometimes a trick move is just what you need to take your opponents by surprise. Some of them can be quite risky, though, so only use them in the attacking third of the field where losing the ball does not put your team in too much danger. Some of these tricks are easy to perform and others need quite a lot of practice.

THE BACKHEEL PASS

To do a backheel pass, you kick the ball back with your heel, or sometimes your sole. You can completely surprise your opponents if you do it quickly, and if there is a team-mate behind you to receive it.

For a basic backheel pass, keep your foot level as you kick so that it doesn't jab down at the ball.

To get a different angle or to disguise your movements, you can cross one leg over the other.

You can roll the ball back with your sole. Point your toes down and kick the middle of the ball.

THE CHEST PASS

Sometimes, when the ball comes at you from a high angle, you have very little time to control it before passing it. You can use your chest to redirect it, but only if the ball is travelling fast - your chest will tend to cushion a slow ball.

Tense your chest muscles and stick your chest out to make a hard surface for the ball to bounce off. Redirect it to a team-mate by turning quickly to the left or right as it reaches you.

This player cannot step back to receive the ball at a lower angle.

This team-mate is not as closely marked, so he is in a good position to receive the ball and play it away.

THE OVERHEAD KICK

This is a spectacular and exciting kick, but it is also very risky. Never try it in the defending third of the field, or in a crowded area where you might kick someone. Also, remember that if you fall you cannot follow up your pass, so make sure other players can follow it up instead.

1. The ball should be at about head height. Take off on one leg, jumping backwards.

2. Keep your eye on the ball and swing your kicking foot up over head height.

At the highest point of the kick, your foot is at other players' head height. This means you need to be especially careful not to kick someone.

3. At the highest point of your jump, strike the ball with your instep.

Try to kick the ball through the middle.

4. Cushion your fall by relaxing and rolling on your shoulder. This will stop you from hurting your wrists.

VARIATIONS

If the ball is not quite as high, you can do overhead kicks while keeping your non-kicking foot on the ground. Lift your kicking foot up to reach the ball, keeping your arms out for balance.

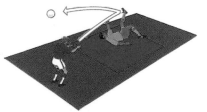

If the ball is further away from you, try the 'scissors' kick. It is a bit like the side volley (see page 11), but you jump and kick while you are sideways on in the air.

HOW TO PRACTISE

Practise on soft grass or a cushioned mat. Get a friend to help you and stand about 5m (15ft) apart. Your friend throws the ball to you for you to kick.

At first, work on landing safely. Once you are sure about this, work on timing your jump, because timing is the main secret of success.

WHAT MAKES A GOOD PASS?

Good passing is not just about mastering clever passes or trick moves. A good pass has to be useful to your team. This means that you need to look around you and think before you pass, then use a pass that is best for the situation - even if it is the simplest one you know.

ACCURACY

Accurate passing between team-mates makes it much more difficult for opponents to intercept the ball. It also saves time, because the player receiving it can take it forward straight away.

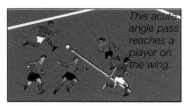

This acute angle pass reaches a player on the wing.

Direction is the first key to accuracy. Try to place the ball where it can be easily collected by your team-mate.

A defender has managed to intercept this short pass.

Pace is important, too. If your pass is too soft an opponent will intercept it. Make sure it is hard enough.

This pass has gone out of play.

Try not to pass the ball too hard, either. If you do, it will be difficult to control and may go too far.

CHOOSING YOUR KICK

There is no such thing as the 'right' kick to use, because each situation is different. However these are some general points to bear in mind before you pass.

Direction of play

1. Check who is free to receive the ball. A carefully selected pass up the field is better than a powerful kick to no one in particular.

This player is free to take a low drive up the pitch.

2. Low, direct passes tend to save time and be more accurate. Only use a high pass to clear the ball over other players' heads.

Here, a low pass is followed by a chip to clear an opponent.

3. If you are in a difficult situation, choose a pass that you can carry out easily. This is better than giving the ball away.

This player uses a simple push pass.

FOOLING YOUR OPPONENTS

You can create opportunities for your team by distracting or confusing your opponents, and by making it difficult for them to guess where the ball will go.

1. Disguise your intentions by pretending to kick the ball in a different direction before you pass.

The player with the ball pretends to pass to the right, then passes straight up the field.

The defender starts to move in the wrong direction.

2. Try not to choose an obvious pass. Pass to someone unmarked or beyond defenders.

This player is a good choice.

3. Use all your kicking skills to make the direction of your pass difficult to anticipate.

This player has used the disguise of a swerve pass to reach a player on the wing.

TIMING

Even if you manage to pass accurately, you can miss your team-mate altogether if you pass at the wrong time. Also, your team-mate is more likely to be able to collect a slightly inaccurate pass if your timing is good.

This player can intercept the pass.

Passing the ball too early gives your opponents the opportunity to run and intercept it.

This defender has caught up with the player in space.

If you wait too long before passing, an opponent may start marking the team-mate who was free.

TIPS FOR SUCCESS

★ Practise all the different kicks so that you are confident enough to try any of them.

★ Look around you as you play so that you can make the best use of any opportunities to pass.

★ Communicate with your team-mates. Shout to each other or use hand signals to attract attention.

PASSING TACTICS

Tactics can mean the special team formations that you plan out before a game. They can also be the moves and decisions you make because of the position you are in on the field, or the ways that you work with other players to get the ball away from your opponents.

PLAYING IN DEFENCE

As a defender, your prioritiy is keeping the ball out of danger. This often means passing it forward, using long drives and volleys to send the ball up the pitch or over attackers' heads.

Defender A has two options. He can pass forward to B or across to C. He chooses to pass to B, which is the best thing to do. If he had passed to C, the ball would not be any further up the field.

Direction out of defence

Defender A uses a low drive to send the ball safely up the pitch, then follows to support B.

A good defender only passes the ball back when he has no alternative. Here, A is surrounded. He passes back to a supporting player (B) who is in a better position to play the ball up the field to C.

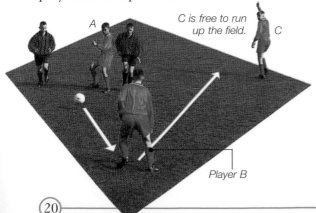

C is free to run up the field.

Player B

ATTACKING PLAY

If you are playing further up the field, you can take more risks. You need to play quickly to confuse defenders, using all the tricks and different passes possible to cut a path through to the goal.

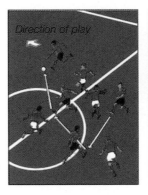

Direction of play

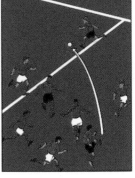

Here, very rapid play using short push passes and volleys gets the ball past defenders.

Play in the middle of the field can get very cramped. Spread the play by passing out to the wing.

Try to pass the ball beyond defenders, especially to players who are in a good position to shoot.

Take defenders by surprise by turning to pass the ball in an unexpected direction or difficult angle.

WALL PASSES

Wall passes are also known as one-two passes. Just before an opponent tackles you, pass the ball quickly to a team-mate, then run around your opponent before he has time to recover. Your team-mate acts as a 'wall'. He passes the ball back to you quickly and you take it forwards up the field.

This player is the wall for the ball to bounce off.

Use wall passes in the attacking third of the field to dodge around defenders.

Run forward quickly to collect your team-mate's pass.

CROSS-OVER PLAYS

This tactic uses a short outside foot pass to do two things. You bring two opponents together, creating space for your own team. You also change the path of the ball before they realize what you have done.

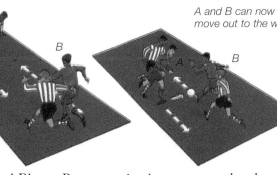

A

B

A and B can now move out to the wings.

A   *B*

Player A and Player B are both being marked. Player A has the ball. A and B run towards each other, taking their markers with them.

As they cross each other, A quickly passes the ball to B with the outside of his foot. The markers are confused and get left behind.

THINKING AHEAD

In order to make your team's tactics effective, keep thinking ahead. Check the position of players around you to work out what they will do next. This will help you to decide what to do, too.

Here, Portugal's Luis Figo has escaped Neil Lennon of Northern Ireland, and is looking up to work out his next move.

SUPPORT PLAY

Supporting means helping your team-mates when you don't have the ball yourself. Each player only has the ball for a small part of each soccer match, so what he does for the rest of the time is very important for his team's success.

FINDING SPACE

Another term for finding space is 'running off the ball'. It means escaping opponents and getting into an open space so that team-mates can pass to you. Opponents may soon catch up, so you need to keep moving into different positions.

It can be tempting to run towards the ball even if a team-mate has it. Try not to do this. Think about where he could pass to, and run there instead.

This player makes a sudden run between the two defenders.

The player with the ball will be able to pass forward to the right of the defenders.

DUMMY RUNS

A 'dummy run' means running into a good position, but then not receiving a pass. It is a way of fooling opponents into running away from the ball.

One kind of dummy run is making your marker think you are about to receive the ball, then letting it run on to a team-mate.

CREATING GOOD ANGLES

'Creating a good angle' refers to how useful your supporting position is. A good angle is one where your team-mate can see you and where you are in a good position for him to pass to.

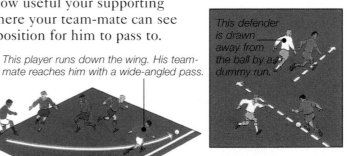

Direction of play

Here, the player runs for a forward pass.

This player runs down the wing. His team-mate reaches him with a wide-angled pass.

This defender is drawn away from the ball by a dummy run.

Always try to place yourself where your team-mate can pass forwards, not across.

A wide-angled pass is less easy to predict, and is more likely to split your opponents' defence.

Another dummy is turning away from the ball, taking a defender with you, so that your team-mate can run forward.

'PASS AND MOVE'

It is always exciting when you have possession of the ball. However, as soon as you pass it on to another player, you need to start supporting again straight away. Always move to follow up your pass, or to find another good supporting position.

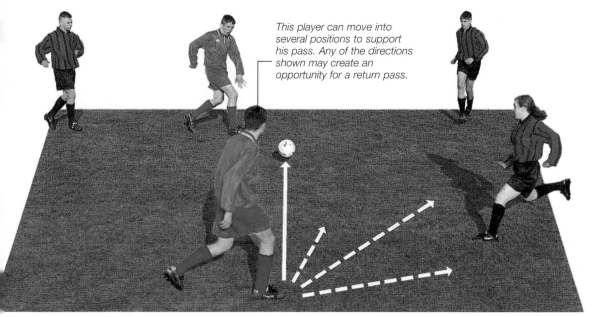

This player can move into several positions to support his pass. Any of the directions shown may create an opportunity for a return pass.

PASS AND MOVE EXERCISE

This exercise helps you to get into the habit of following up your passes. You need three or more players. Divide up into two opposite rows.

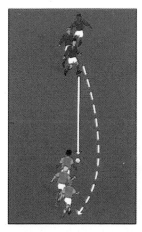 

The first player in one row passes to the first in the other, then runs to the end of the opposite row.

The player at the front of that row passes back and follows the ball. Carry on like this.

SUPPORT GAME

This game is best played by seven players, two defenders (labelled D) and five attackers (A). As you play, use the support skills that you have learned. Run off the ball to find space, work out the best kick to use before passing and follow up your passes.

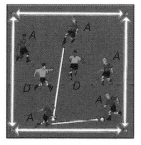 

Mark out a pitch about 20m (60ft) square. You need one ball. The As have the ball and try to pass to each other without the Ds intercepting.

If a D manages to intercept, he swaps places with the A player who passed. If the As manage ten passes in a row, the Ds swap with two As anyway.

HEADING IN ATTACK

Using headers in attack or to go for goal is one of the most exciting elements of the game. It often means taking advantage of split-second opportunities, so you have to be courageous, take risks and really attack the ball.

DOWNWARD HEADERS

When heading for goal, you should try to keep the ball down to make it more difficult for goalkeepers to save. To make the ball go down when you head it, you need to get above it to hit the top part of it, then nod your head down firmly as you make contact.

1. To catch the top part of the ball with your forehead, you often have to jump.

2. As you would for any header, try to keep your eyes open all the time.

3. As you head the ball away, push forwards and down with your forehead.

DIVING HEADERS

Usually, you use a diving header to try for goal. This is a very dramatic way of scoring, but bear in mind that once you have committed yourself you will be on the ground and unable to play another move until you get up again.

This player watches where the ball has gone. He must now get up quickly in case he needs to follow it up.

Approach a diving header with plenty of speed. This will add to its power.

Keep your eyes on the ball and dive forwards, letting your legs leave the ground.

Direct the ball to the left or right by turning your head as you make contact.

As you hit the ground, try to relax your body so that you don't hurt yourself.

HEADING PRACTICE

This is a practice for three players. Mark out a goal 6m (18ft) across. Place a marker 15m (45ft) in front of it. One player is the goalkeeper.

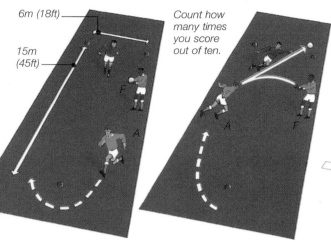

6m (18ft)

15m (45ft)

Count how many times you score out of ten.

One player (F) stands at the side of the goal. The other (A) stands between the goal and the marker. A runs around the marker as F throws the ball to him.

A has to dash for the ball and head at goal. F should vary the height of the ball for A to try different headers. Rotate players after ten goes.

FLICK-ON HEADERS

There is one exception to the rule of using your forehead when heading, and that is when you let the ball glance off the top of your head. You usually do this to lift the ball out of the reach of a defender, to a team-mate who may be able to shoot.

As the ball passes over you, jump straight into the air and let it glance off your head. It carries on in basically the same direction, though you can direct it left or right slightly.

THROW-HEAD-CATCH GAME

This game is for eight or more players. Divide into two teams. Each team has a goal and goalkeeper. Everyone else marks a player from the other team. To play, you must follow the sequence 'throw, head, catch', even when you intercept the ball. You can only score a goal with a header.

SHOOTING TO SCORE

Once you have mastered all the different kicking techniques and passing skills, you have all the basic skills that you need for shooting, too. However there are several things to bear in mind which can make a big difference to the number of goals you score.

WHAT WILL HELP YOU TO SCORE?

Try to keep the ball low. It is easier for a goalkeeper to stretch for a high ball than to reach down for a low one.

Aim at the far corners of the goal. The goalkeeper can more easily save shots which come straight at him.

Vary your approach to goal. If you always take the same approach, defenders will be likely to intercept you.

Shoot whenever you have the chance. Go for risky shots. It's better to have a go and miss than not to have a go at all.

Try not to look in the direction you are going to shoot. This makes your shot too easy to anticipate.

Practise shooting from an acute angle. Angled shots are difficult to anticipate and to save.

ACCURACY

You may think you need power to be shoot effectively. It is true that hard shots are difficult to save, but they are also difficult to control. There is no point in a hard shot if you miss, so it is better to work on your accuracy first.

26

REBOUND SHOTS

When you shoot, don't stop to see what happens. The ball may hit the post, or the goalkeeper may drop the ball.

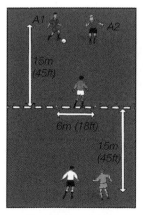

If you keep moving and follow your shot in towards the goal, you can shoot again if the ball rebounds.

WHEN NOT TO SHOOT

Whenever you can see a clear path to goal you should try a shot. Sometimes, though, it's not so clear and a team-mate may have a better chance of scoring than you. Then, it is better to pass than to shoot.

This player has a clear view of the goal and could easily shoot.

TARGET PRACTICE

The best way to improve your shooting is to practise aiming at a target. You can do this by marking a target on a wall to shoot at, but it is even better to practise against a goalkeeper. This exercise is for five players. It should improve your speed and accuracy.

Keep the shots as low as possible

Aim for the corners of the goal

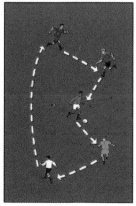

Mark out a goal 6m (18ft) wide. Stand in pairs, 15m (45ft) in front of and behind the goalkeeper.

A1 passes to A2, who tries to shoot. A1 becomes a defender and tries to stop him.

The ball now goes across to the B players who follow the same pattern. B2 tries to score.

Next, swap around as shown and play until everyone has had ten shots. The best score out of ten wins.

APPROACHES TO GOAL

To improve their chances of scoring, attackers need different strategies to outwit the goalkeeper and defenders. These are some you can use, on your own or working with team-mates, to create good shooting opportunities as you reach the attacking third of the field.

CROSSING THE BALL

As a general rule you should try to pass the ball forward. Sometimes, however, it can be effective to pass the ball across, when you are on the wing in the attacking third - you can pass it to a team-mate so that he can shoot. This is called crossing the ball.

This player is in a good position to try a header.

By using a long, high cross, this player sends the ball across the goalmouth.

Use a variety of passes to get the ball into the penalty area, so that a team-mate can shoot as it crosses in front of the goal.

Once you have decided to cross the ball, cross it as soon as possible before defenders can take up good positions.

Make sure there is a team-mate to make use of your cross. There is no point in crossing the ball straight to a defender or the goalkeeper.

SHOOTING FROM CROSSES

Check the position of other team-mates. If you clash over the same cross a good chance may be lost.

If a defender is marking you, try to dodge him just as your team-mate crosses the ball.

Act really quickly when you see the opportunity to score and don't be put off by your opponents. Dash for the ball and have a go at a shot. Try to shoot down with a diving or downwards header, or a volley.

DRAWING THE GOALKEEPER OUT

Goalkeepers often come out of goal as you approach, because this narrows down the area you can shoot at.

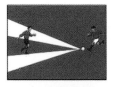

Here, it is difficult for the goalkeeper to cover the big areas that you can shoot at.

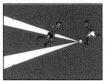

As he moves out the areas get smaller, but there is now a big space behind him.

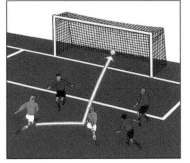

If you can, use this opportunity to pass to a team-mate out to the side so that he can shoot.

Even if the goalkeeper jumps at the right time, he will not be able to reach this high chip over his head.

You could also try chipping the ball, lifting it over the goalkeeper's head as he approaches and down into the goal. Make sure you send the ball high enough.

TURN AND SHOOT

There are often times when your back is to the goal. By turning to shoot quickly, you may take defenders by surprise. This exercise helps you practise this. It is for four players - a goalkeeper, a defender and two attackers.

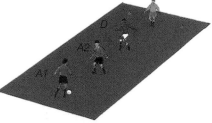

Mark out a goal. One attacker (A1) faces the goal. The other (A2) has his back to the goal and the defender (D) stands behind him.

You could use a wall pass.

A1 passes to A2, who has to turn quickly. A1 is now a supporting player, so A2 can pass to him or shoot. D tries to stop him scoring.

The players have now swapped roles.

Here, A2 shoots as soon as he receives the ball.

Take it in turns to be the attackers. You could play as two teams of two and see which side does best as the attacking team.

ATTACKING PLAY

When your team has the ball, you are in attack, whatever your position. To play a good attacking game, you combine all the skills you have learned with a positive attitude and the determination to win. These two pages should help you develop the competitive edge that you need to do this.

FOUR PASS DRILL

To play this game, you need to use quick and varied passing skills. You need a big group - fourteen is best, but you could play with a few less or a few more. Mark out a pitch 50m (150ft) long and 30m (90ft) wide. Divide it into three equal areas.

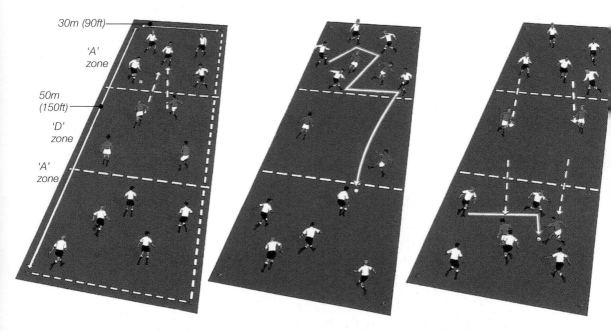

30m (90ft)

'A' zone

50m (150ft)

'D' zone

'A' zone

1. Get into two groups of five attackers (A) and one group of four defenders (D). The Ds go into the middle zone, the As into the end zones. One A group has the ball.

2. These As pass the ball to each other four times while two of the defenders try to stop them. If the As succeed, they pass the ball over the D area to the other A team.

3. The other two defenders go into the other A area as the As try for four passes. If a D intercepts the ball at any time, he takes the place of the A who passed.

PASSING REMINDER TIPS

★ Communicate with your team-mates so that they know where to pass to.

★ If you don't have the ball, support by running around to find space.

★ Choose passes that you know you can carry out accurately.

★ Make use of wall passes and cross-over plays to dodge defenders.

★ Hold your pass until a team-mate is in a position to receive it.

★ Unless you want to clear defenders, keep your passes as low as possible.

SMALL-PITCH SHOOTING GAME

The area that you have for this game is very confined, so you have to make quick decisions and try to shoot as much as possible.

Goal

30m (90ft)

20m (60ft)

Mark out a pitch 20m (60ft) long and 30m (90ft) wide, and mark out two goals. You need at least ten players, in even numbers if possible.

Divide into two teams with a goalkeeper each. One goalkeeper starts the game each time by kicking the ball into the middle.

Here, one team has passed just twice before shooting.

Keep moving around to find good shooting positions.

Players from each team mark each other closely. Each team is only allowed up to three passes before trying a shot at goal.

If no one tries a shot after three consecutive passes, the ball goes over to the other team. Keep a record of the score.

STAR SHOT

Being an attacker or striker takes lots of determination and courage. If you watch star players, you will see that they do not hesitate to take opportunities to go for the ball and shoot.

This is Brazilian attacker Juninho playing at full stretch in a match against Sweden.

SHOOTING REMINDER TIPS

★ Always have a go if you see an opportunity. Don't worry that you might miss.

★ Vary your shots. Try shots from difficult angles, not just in front of the goal.

★ Keep alert when your team shoots. There may be a rebound opportunity.

★ Use crosses to make opportunities for diving headers and volleys.

★ Keep the ball down and aim for the bottom corners of the goal.

★ Make your shots accurate rather than powerful.

INDEX

If you would like to improve your soccer by attending a soccer course
in your holidays, you can find out about different courses from:

Bobby Charlton International Ltd
Hopwood Hall, Rochdale Road
Middleton, Manchester M24 6XH
Tel: 0161 643 3113

This edition first published in 2006 by Usborne
Publishing Ltd., 83-85 Saffron Hill, London
EC1N 8RT, England. www.usborne.com
Copyright © 1996, 2002, 2006 Usborne Publishing Ltd